*Dance and
Disappear*

Dance and Disappear

Laura Kasischke

University of Massachusetts Press
Amherst and Boston

Library of Congress Cataloging-in-Publication Data

Kasischke, Laura, 1961–
  Dance and disappear / Laura Kasischke.
     p. cm.
"Winner of the Associated Writing Programs
  2001 award in short fiction"
ISBN 1-55849-352-2 (alk. paper)
I. Title.
PS3561.A6993 D36 2002
811'.54—dc21

2002000720

British Library Cataloguing in Publication data are available *for my B, L, and J*

Acknowledgments

Grateful acknowledgment is made to the editors of the following journals in which these poems first appeared

Fine Madness: "Laura"
The Iowa Review: "Bike Ride with Older Boys,"
    "Small Boys Petting Caterpillar"
The Kenyon Review: "Clown"
The Missouri Review: "Buffalo," "Grace," "Mud"
The New England Review: "Executioner as Muse"
The Southern Review: "Day," "Joy"

"Bike Ride with Older Boys" was reprinted in the
    Pushcart Prize: Best of the Small Presses, 2001.
"Grace," "Oven," and "Please" were published in *The New
    American Poets: A Breadloaf Anthology, 2000.*

Here lies the body of Emily Wright;
She signaled left, and then turned right

Epitaph

Contents

One

~

Two

~

Three

~

Dance and
Disappear

one

Kitchen Song

The white bowls in the orderly
cupboards filled with nothing.

The sound
of applause in running water.
All those who've drowned in oceans, all
who've drowned in pools, in ponds, the small
family together in the car hit head on. The pantry

full of lilies, the lobsters scratching to get out of the pot, and
    God

being pulled across the heavens
in a burning car.

The recipes
like confessions.
The confessions like songs.
The sun. The bomb. The white

bowls in the orderly
cupboards filled with blood. *I wanted*

something simple, and domestic. A kitchen song.

They were just driving along. Dad
turned the radio off, and Mom
turned it back on.

Day

It was a day—a bit
of camouflage cloth
through which the sun could shine.
I decided to hang the laundry

on a line. It was another day
in my civilian life. Monday, the day

of lost keys. Tuesday the breathing sweetness
of macaroni and cheese. When I

heard my son's sheets slapping
at the breeze, I turned around.

The sound
of soldiers
marching through the trees.

Wednesday

is the sparrow's day, she
nests in the place where the shingles
have broken away from the eaves
in a home she's made for herself

out of Kleenex
and twigs.

The bus
is yellow.
It goes and comes

bearing the small
laundry of my son.

Thursday, a star
falls out of the sky as I
wheel the child's bike
to the garage—the garage, which is a darkness
like the father

of my son, glittering
with wrenches, the smell of rags and oil. He keeps

a hat he wore in the jungle
hanging from a nail on the door. Friday

the clouds
part above the highway, leaving
a ragged hole
in my clean sky. The laundry

on the line, how like our lives! As if

something of ourselves
could be left behind, hanging

in the sun, taking
our places, bearing
our vague shapes
long after we've stepped away, wearing

other lives on other days. *Shadows, pants,* on Saturdays

the library's stone lions run
freely through the streets.
We have to lock the doors.
We have to stay inside. But

by Sunday morning, they've come back, and see

how emptily they stand
very still and very quiet

side by side, side by side

Buffalo

I had the baby in my arms, he was asleep.
We were waiting for Old Faithful, who was late
The tourists smelled like flowers, or

like shafts of perfume moving
from bench to bench, from
Gift Shop to Port-o-Pot. The sun

was a fluid smear in the sky, like
white hair in water. The women
were as beautiful as the men, who

were so beautiful they never needed
to see their wives or children again.

It happened then.

Something underground. The hush of sound.

I remembered
once pretending
to have eaten a butterfly.
My mother held my arms hard until
I told her it was a lie

and then she sighed. I've

loved every minute of my life!
The day I learned to ride a bike
without training wheels, I

might as well have been riding a bike
with no wheels at all! If

at any time, I'd

had to agree to bear
twenty-seven sorrows
for a single one of these joys . . .

If the agreement were that I
had to love it all so much
just, in the end, to die . . .

Still, I can taste those wings I didn't eat, the sweet
and tender lavender of them. One

tourist covered her mouth
with a hand
and seemed to cry. How

could I have doubted her?
There were real tears in her eyes! The daisies

fell from her dress, and if
at that moment
she'd cracked an egg in a bowl,

the bowl would have filled with light. If

there is a God, why not

this violent froth, this
huge chiffon scarf
of pressure under water under her
white sandals in July?

The baby was asleep, still sucking, in my arms, a lazy

wand of sun moved
back and forth across his brow. I heard a girl's laughter
in the parking lot, soft
and wild as

the last note of "Jacob's Ladder"
played by the children's handbell choir.

I turned around.

It had been watching me. Or him. Or both of us.

Good beast, I whispered to it
facetiously under my breath.
It took, in our direction, one

slow and shaggy step.

Clown

It was summer, and the clown had come
to the same restaurant to which we'd come
for a piece of strawberry pie.
Big white smile.
Wig of fire.

The sun had begun to set
with a piece of gold in its mouth.
There were devils in the dumpsters eating flies.
What's that? the three year old asked.
I said, *She is a clown.*

Time had begun to pass so fast I felt
as if the weekly newspaper came to our house every day, yet
I had a photograph of myself
in which I'd blown my bangs back, wanting
to have wings like an angel, or Farrah Fawcett

when what I had was hair
that made me look in this photograph
like a girl who'd lived for a while
in another century, on a distant planet.
Someday my children would laugh.

She's not a woman, the three year old said
of the clown. There were
white seeds blowing around in the evening breeze
without a plan, landing their fluff-craft in
the Big Boy parking lot, onto the hoods of cars.

A man puts a gun to your head and demands
your child, what should you do? That's
the kind of early summer night it was.
The kind of night in which, perhaps,
you have a last moment

to look around and laugh—at
the child, and the clown, and the pie, and the fact
that if each atom could be collapsed
into a sphere no bigger than its core, all
of the Washington Monument could be crammed

into a space no bigger than an eraser.
How modest were your desires!
In the order of things, it's true
a clown is last, but all of us are futile
when it comes to want

and stupid to look at in a restaurant.

Spontaneous Human Combustion

I. An Introduction

She was waiting for her husband in the kitchen (cup
of coffee, slice of chiffon pie) when he came in tossing
beneath his burning hair. A thing like this can happen

to anyone, anywhere

but especially in the West, full
as it is
of dreaming and fading, and

especially in the U.S.
where we have become child-
like strangers in in the place we've made.

The basement
full of batteries and cables. Outside,
the magnolia full of snow.
It was winter, they were older, all

her little phobias—

sinusitis, pneumonia—

when her husband stepped into the kitchen
thrashing around in his new clothes.

II. Documented Cases

Inexplicable incinerations
have always been with us. It isn't
our purpose
to list every instance.
The girl who stepped out of her Home Ec class
in 1967
and was found an hour later
in the stairwell, as ash.
The Countess Cornelia Bendi Ceséna
who went to bed in 1770
feeling 'dull and heavy.'

If one becomes accustomed
to sensational detail
she loses her taste for ordinary things.
Some mornings I wake
with my lips parted, pale

and passionate at the bathroom mirror
with nothing left to say. Too

many lies, pains
in my legs. During

the trial of O.J.,
I was pregnant
in Las Vegas, and couldn't

tear myself away. Maybe

I wanted something
hotter than the sun
to step through the broken gate
and carry me away.

The weeds have teeth, unlike the daisies.
A curious calm at the center of the flames.
One burning bird in flight
is enough to set the whole country on fire

An example or two will have to suffice.

III. A History

There are places and times in which people become
more combustible than others. I've stood

in forests
at the edges of suburbs
and felt a careless crowd
tossing matches in my heart.

Someone has left a cup
of grape juice above the fridge. Like

a woman drunk on Eau
de Cologne, waiting
there for weeks, this
juice has become

something purer than it ever should have been.

The Listerine like cognac.
The Bactine like gin.

Let them hide the key to the liquor cabinet,
I'll just go to the bathroom and lock myself in.

Believe me, the heat
itself
is simple, deep
inside the body. No one
but the victim can feel it, but when

you open your mouth
to say something nice,
the sweetness of your own vineyard on the hillside in the summer

set on fire floats out.

IV. Girl, Kissing, Bursts into Flames

It happened to me, I was there. Out

past the factory, where

whole pleasure could be pried
open with an impulse and a wrench. The strange

cowboy of him, chains
and leather and mascara.
I was a keychain, some patchy fog.
The noise of the neural system seemed
to be coming from the stars.

Oh, the wren brought those kisses down from heaven
A screech-owl brought them up from hell.
Oh earth, wind, water, this

is a simile not satisfied by fire—

still, if he'd doused me in kerosene that night
I could not have burned better or brighter.

Grace

Who can tell the difference between the state
of grace and the state of inebriation? Who

can tell the difference between love-drunk
and just drunk? Once

I turned around too fast
at a party with a drink in my hand
and splashed the shoes of a man, who said,

"Don't tell me. Let me guess. Your name is Grace."

Whether it's night or day
is a matter of indifference to the sun. Who cares

what year it was, what month, whether
the couple asleep on the park bench
in one another's arms
are lovers, or drunks? They claimed

the *Hindenburg* was lighter than air.
Everything balanced—

the lift of the hydrogen, the weight of the ballast, a battleship
    made

out of shadow, and linen,
an emptiness like elegance
over the Atlantic, which was nothing

but a glossy magazine, open. Oh, *there they go*, I imagined

the other people at this party
whispered to each other
as we wandered with our cocktails to the lawn. Imagine

that dirigible passing over
at this moment. Diamond rings, false teeth, swastikas—

all the little baggage
with which people travel. Imagine it as grace: that

moment just before
the moment in which the mystery
would like to speak to us

if we would like to listen, in which

pure pleasure, its
huge kind surge, could
pick us up together, speak

to us in human terms. The music
like honey. The temple
full of monkeys. To show us how much greater

is the game than any player.
How much brighter
is the porchlight
than the chalklight inside a moth:

Air pressure.
Air temperature.
The weight of the passengers.
The lift of the oxygen.
Everything balanced.
Everything gauged. But then

the fear of water again—of flight, of public restrooms, of
open spaces, bees,
bridges, traffic, grace. *The Hindenburg*

was landing
when it suddenly became

brighter than the sun at noon.
It had no weight.
In Lakehurst, New Jersey, all the dogs barked
It was Ascension Day.
The month was May.
1937.
A light rain.
The *Hindenburg* was landing.

We all know *nothing*
is lighter than air,
but it sure felt that way.
The papery

disintegration, the star of a girl dropped
onto the world, the bird
tossed right along
with its cage into the flames.

In heaven, the burning skeleton.

For *years* he called me Grace.

Show and Tell

Now begins the season of Minor Feasts.
Easter's over. All
that grief. These

are the first green weeks. May

opens it up to the public—the cathedrals
& boutiques. The tourists

and the dumb animals come, the simple
insects, and the very young—

Beau McCallister is back. Beau

who brought to Show and Tell
the news of his grandmother's death.
I see him clearly, still, walking
with his small fists in his pockets, face

made out of tears and phlegm, taking
his child-sized seat again.

White-blond hair.
Big square teeth.

I was also a child then
but when my grandmother died
it hadn't occurred to me to tell. Outside,
the willow
facetiously weeped. The sloppy

needlepoint of lilacs in the breeze. Soon
a hard rain would come
to drive nails and needles into the ground

And here's another thing we don't yet know:
In another decade, Beau

will die a boy's swift death
by Jeep. He will

be driving too
fast in the snow, too
close to the side of the road. And this

old lady in France
taking bad snapshots of the stained glass (*Grandma,*

there's too much light, step back)—this
shadow in the corner of her last bright blur

will belong to me.

Green Bicycle

There it is on the horizon, wavering.
There it goes, disappearing, into space.

My father hears sounds in the basement.
He goes downstairs in his underwear, a seventy
year-old man in the static of night and rain.

The wall's caved in. He turns
and climbs the stairs again.

No trouble, no illumination.
I guess God likes it that way.
But the foundation of my father's
house has collapsed
and the insurance company won't pay
and here we stand this afternoon

stupefied in our wet shoes.

No enemies, no friends.
Without the middle, no beginning or end.
If the phone doesn't ring, if the thing never breaks

The world says, Give me
more of yourself than you can spare
and I'll take you to a strange
city, drop you off downtown, then

come to pick you up a little later, greatly changed.

Once, an old man

sat down beside me on a park bench.
He said he was from Ireland.
There were thistles
in the wastefield beside the pond, pre-

historic in their silence, their
shapes, their faith. My bike
was green, and new, and mine. I owned

the most beautiful bike I'd ever seen
and rode it, watching
myself ride it
like a prepubescent ghost
with long soft hair
into the supermarket's plate glass window.

It had gotten me to the place
I was, which was, perhaps, further

than I ever should have been.

He put his hand on my hand, leaned
over and tried

to kiss me on the lips.

Oh my God, I said—got up, ran, never looked back.

But today I would ask that old man, *What about all that?*

The turtles were paddling on the pond's smooth murk
poking up their faces for a better look.
The thistles made their hushes
in the breezes. *Tell me, kiss me, Old One. This*

time it'll be
our little secret. Though

that time, thrilled
with my first terror, riding
my bike home
I stopped

over and over to tell everyone I knew,

and my father, a very young man,
came down there looking for you.

two

Executioner as Muse

I am Schmidt, who was the son
of a hangman, who
like every other boy
believed for a while that my mind
was the pure white flower of my spine.
I lived. I died. I became

a glimpse of your own face in the window of a train, passing
the barns on fire, the steeples slickened by the rain. I became

a long stripe down the center of the highway
in the middle of the night, leading you into the accident
of someone else's life.

I cannot be buried
because I am always alive.

Like rocks at the bottom of moving water
I have been liberated from my shape—can waver, can climb
the stairs you climb each night,

right behind you, stomping
all over the moonlight
in your little silver shoes, locking
the door to your room.

Pick up the pen, and I am you:
Schmidt, the son of a hangman, who
became a hangman, too.

Joy

I stayed in bed for days and watched
a spider in the light spin
an airy web above my head, something

cool and loose, without
the use of force, or weight.

That time, I nearly died

of joy. I was a child. Still alive.
Relatives stood above me smiling. Summer
was my sickness. Translucent

nurses brought me everything
I needed, while I

swam in and out of sun, which
unraveled its white knitting
on the surface of the pool, and flew

above the orchards, which stretched
in bloom
from my mind to the end time—just
above the branches, but at great speed

and thought I saw a small girl running
like a madwoman beneath the trees.

I didn't even need to eat! I *drank* the beautiful meals
my mother made for me

from coolness and silver spoons. My father

sat at the edge of the bed
and prayed for the angels' protection. Like

talcum and masculine sweat, the smell
of wet feathers as I slept. I got better

and better, listening . . .

But what was that sound? The clock? The toilet

flushing? Rain on the playground? The ocean
choking on its own waves?

No.

It was a dog
lapping at a bloody tray.

Childhood came and went in a day

and I woke on Sunday in the arms of a stranger.
Oh, I realized then,

this must be joy again. Despite

the headache, the salty thirst, the shame—that

spinning above the bed, more
light than thread, was

exactly, *exactly,* the same.

The Visibility of Spirits

Those ancients placed much confidence in the reality of the spirit world
by which they felt themselves surrounded. Man believed in an other-worldly
order of existence because from time to time he met its representative

in his own world.This morning

the breeze is so fresh it's like a knife pulled
cleanly from the center
of a perfectly baked pie. The children

want pancakes for breakfast. *The skillet*
is ready, the Bisquick box says, *when*

a few drops of water sprinkled on it
dance and disappear. There is

a flower stuck into
a Diet Coke can on the counter. Or

maybe it's a weed. I plucked her after summer had already

set her on fire with his
blazing rages and ennui. Now

her face is orange, her eye is brown. At

the center of the brownness
there's a sound, a whispered rattle made

out of self-
pity and despair. *It isn't fair.*

Once, lying naked
beside my husband in a sweaty
bed, an awful

moth flew through an open window
and landed on my breast. It had

come from outer-space and still
had star-chalk on its face. I felt

so stunned and sure of something
I couldn't wave it away. *Hello? Hello in there I say. Who*

were you, and what happened? She looked at me
with her hairy eyes, and seemed to say, I don't

remember, and yet
I live and have
these wings for awhile, and my
girlish figure, and my
beauty queen smile. Oh

my God, I said, though I

hadn't taken the Lord's
name in vain
for a long time. And then,

Jesus Christ, Jesus Christ, Jesus Christ.

Laura

Some nights, washing dishes,
she'd catch a glimpse of them together

reflected in the kitchen
window, and she'd think *Who are we?* Then

through the shiver
of the ornamental cherry tree she'd see

the neighbors in their own
kitchen window lit with light, and that
other wife

moving through her rooms
carrying a brilliant spoon, and that

other husband pausing
in the center
of her movement, posing
with his cigarette behind

the small black-hearted leaves, lost

in the ornamental blossoms—and they

were not the strangers to her, their

lives were not the mystery. The sky
above them all—that sky! So

many stars floating
above the stuff.

Sputnik,
Vanguard,
Challenger. Radio

waves bouncing from
one bright piece
of junk to another. And the dishes

filled with voices

in their own backyards.

And still, such silence, you could have sucked it. Just
a bit of rustling. The leaves

between them, almost nothing.
That wife's spoon, emitting its own light.

That husband's cigarette, like a sun.

Black Car

. . . a country girl who gave birth to a child fourteen days before
Candlemas, at night in the garden of her employer stopped its mouth with
earth and making a hole with her hand buried it while it struggled.
Beheaded

with a sword
for these crimes at Aylsdorf,
May 17, 1594.
A firefly

in her armpit, her mouth, between her legs.
Cradle full of candles, the cellar full of night.

This morning I saw an old woman
emerge from her hotel.

A body of murky water
and not a shiver on it.
She was the old woman
I'd been fearing all my life.
A woman
who had always been polite,
but who had never once been kind.

Once, a black car pulled
into my driveway
and pulled back out.

That afternoon, the sun
was an eye on fire
in the sky.
But it had its headlights on.

I waited all day
for that car to come back,
but it never came.

By twilight, the bracelet at my wrist
had become a silver sigh.
I felt as if I'd spent the day
digging a little hole
in hard dirt with my hand. What

a book would have to be written, I thought then,
to explain the difference

between fear and dread,
guilt and sin, justice
and mercy! I put

my hands to my neck when I heard

the screen door open
and close in the wind.

Oven

The fruit is ruined, but the bread is baked.
The meat is no longer raw
on its tin plate

but where
is the hooded cloak
of a warm summer night, the new lover drunk
in the middle of the day, the possum with its
damp white-hearted face? Or the woman

turned to cinders
one morning at the beach. *She*

was a teenager, wearing
a bikini—
who is this? who is this?

There are chalk
drawings on the walls
but they're so crude. What
can they tell us

of what the birds really tasted
when they pierced the pale blossoms
for the first time with their tongues?

The empty church.
The empty school.
The theater, empty, the play is done.

The oven as womb.
The oven as grave.
So much no one
ever needs to say. All

this singing and saying—for centuries—the same

While inside the oven, not a sound not a sound.
The path leads in, the ashes out.

Kiss

We had gone to the park to kiss, to kiss
one another's lips. It was
the first kiss. It was winter. There was a ship

crossing an ocean
we didn't know existed, and

the ship was sailing toward us

with a cargo of spices
and gold and slaves
and something else
we couldn't name—that

ship was bringing with it
our disease, the one
we'd never heard of, the one
we'd die of sweetly.

Sweetly, we kissed quickly
with our mouths closed.

After years I forget about him, and he
forgets about me. There

is never a path through that damp park. That
park made of memory is always
foggy and gray. The snow

finally melts, but under it all

there's nothing but newspaper, faded
into the lawn and the sidewalk, until

suddenly it's spring. The world
is hard as marble, and green.

His children are screaming in his yard
My children are screaming in mine.
They are children.
They know nothing

but the trances of being children.

When the light is dim
I can see through them
and on the other side, there's him

The Lamb and the Turtle

These are the Muses who once taught Hesiod beautiful song
  as he was pasturing his flock in the foothills of holy Mount Helicon .

One has been taken
Two are left
One is left
Two are gone

Let us wash our little feet in this here silver stream.
Finally, we're free—

And this last one left standing at the foot of my bed, which

one is she? Meditation? Music? Memory? Her

body's tender, but her eyes are dead.
Her body's dead, but her eyes are wild.
An exotic dancer in another life.
A boa, and a smile . . .

Like her, I've let so many others slip off giggling into the
    night—

The Exes and the Great Aunts, the best of my best friends .

See you in heaven, I said. Good-bye, don't cry. We

shall meet again, and recognize
one another by our fingerprints, and memories—
no two alike.

Down at the Animal Shelter tonight

they're putting the stray dogs down.

Bye-bye Rover, Spangles, Spot—

Nameless, Brown, Dog—

Who knows what shelter waits for us beyond this one?

It may be the shelter of dreamless sleep,
or the shelter of endless field.
We only know that if we wake at all,
it won't be here, or we.
Tomorrow there will be
a strange dog in your cage.
Tomorrow there will be no song, thought, memory . . .
And the moment the last one slips away,
the body begins to decay.

Strange how the rocks are made of weight, but what are they?

Hurry. Hide. The peace that passeth under-
standing is headed our way. Hear

the flapping of the wings of her white lab coat in the sky.

This morning the orange juice was so cold it opened
an eye of pain in my mind.
With it I could see
that last Muse watching me.

Grabbed my keys. Got in the SUV. Sped
past an Amish man who didn't look at me. He

didn't need to look at me to know
that I was another woman born
in the decade of Free Love,

schooled in the decade of free drugs,

married in the decade
of the condominium, and in

the decade of presidential sin I bore a son.

He was having trouble with his buggy.
Summer, already, gone and come
like someone whose penis I'd regret having sucked.

Oh my God, I said
to the reflection of my face, Soon I'll be a stranger
in the bed I've made . . .

And this little stew of pills I swallow
with my orange juice in the morning—

it'll kill me in my forties, or it will make me immortal

And then I remembered my mother's advice
as I wept beside her
in her bed at the end of the Oncology Ward—

It will begin to be alright
again when I die.
You'll always love me, but then
you can begin to forget . . .

All my life, my mother's
cheerful and ruinous wisdom, she
fed it to me like pure
sugar from a bitter little spoon.
(Mama, where are you?)

One has been taken
Two are left
One is left
Two have gone on—

One had to do with temperature.
The other with love.
And here I am rubbing lotion

on the cold hands of the other one,

who says, *You know, despite your neglect, the little garden grows.*

In that, a wealth of advice
on how to live this life, or

one good rule on how to begin not to live again.

It's not an easy metaphor
to resist, but which one is?

For a long time I felt that I
was central to my own life, and then
I passed through many years in which
no matter where I was (smiling

into the ice cream or paddling up the Nile) part of me was
        searching through my purse
for spare change, a cigarette, a way to escape that place—

And always a small square of green in the back of my brain—

what Idaho was in my imagination before I'd been to it.

Now, of the three things given to me at birth
I'm left with this.

Now, of the three who were born by my side
one still is.

The gorgeous hubris of it, the staggering
arrogance: I won't quit.

In a cauldron at Delphi the lamb and the turtle simmer.
The two others dip their pale hands in it.

Bruised banana in a basket!
Popsicle melting in her own sky-blue gown
on the kitchen counter! This

is the only feast I managed
in all these years to prepare for you—

Sweet one, last one, dearest
of the three because you couldn't leave.

This is it.
Your feast:

Whatever's left of me.

three

Bike Ride with Older Boys

The one I didn't go on.

I was thirteen,
and they were older.
I'd met them at the public pool. I must

have given them my number. I'm sure

I'd given them my number,
knowing the girl I was . . .

It was summer. My afternoons
were made of time and vinyl.
My mother worked,
but I had a bike. They wanted

to go for a ride.
Just me and them. I said
okay fine, I'd
meet them at the Stop-n-Go
at four o'clock.
And then I didn't show.

I have been given a little gift—
something sweet
and inexpensive, something
I never worked or asked or said
thank you for, most
days not aware
of what I have been given, or what I missed—

because it's that, too, isn't it?
I never saw those boys again.
I'm not as dumb
as they think I am

but neither am I wise. Perhaps

it is the best
afternoon of my life. Two
cute and older boys
pedaling beside me—respectful, awed.When we

turn down my street, the other girls see me . . .

Everything as I imagined it would be.

Or, I am in a vacant field. When I
stand up again, there are bits of glass and gravel
ground into my knees.
I will never love myself again.
Who knew then
that someday I would be

thirty-seven, wiping
crumbs off the kitchen table with a sponge,
    remembering
them, thinking
of this—

those boys still waiting
outside the Stop-n-Go, smoking
cigarettes, growing older.

Guide to Imaginary Places

1. Abaton

Never to forget that moment:

We had just stepped out of the plane
and into the air, and the seagulls
were screaming around us, wild

white gloves, demanding
something from us

because we were harmless, alive, and there. Something

entered my heart then, like a curse
or a prayer. I closed my eyes

and cast out a net through which
every other minute
in my life passed.

It was an imaginary net . . . .

It is not an accessible place.
Glimpsed on the horizon, it fills the one who sees it
with sorrow like the vague

childhood memory
of linen drying on a line. Once

the most beautiful blue-eyed cat I'd ever seen
bit my hand with a viciousness

I never knew beauty had. I bled.

I never spoke
to my mother again
after the day my mother died. Never even tried

Sir Thomas Bulfinch said
he saw the outline of it
while traveling from Glasgow to Troon.

He mentioned a distant music
in his memoirs, music
somewhat like the sun

shining through a thin green leaf

of lettuce in the air, but music

seems unlikely. The name
of the place in Greek means
You can't go there.

II. Back of the North Wind

I've never been,
but once I was given a prescription for it
and I still have the pills

in the medicine chest, in case.
They say it's always May.
Never any rain—

though the citizens look a little sad
as if they're waiting to be happier someday. Don't

bother to ask how they got that way. It's all

roads, crossroads, roadside benches. If you ask for directions, what

can they say? Only

one drunken bus driver
has ever gone and come back. He claimed

that time passed very slowly. That

the time it took to wink
at a girl

lasted twenty days. He

couldn't quite remember
its location, but
thought perhaps he'd found it

in a dense forest in Brittany, or
somewhere in central Africa, or
on an extensive peninsula off
the coast of California, discovered

by a Spaniard in 1703.

They're always healthy.
They wear crowns. There's

a tree at the center of the town, which
if climbed to the top
is tall enough

to look back at the rest of the world, and see—

nothing but a bit of mountain
pushing out of the ocean, casting

a long, monotonous shadow on the water

between where we are and where we wanted to be

III. The Past

It's in the air between the cards
when the deck is shuffled. Even

a diamond's mostly space, or so the physicists say,

and we all know the body's mostly water. One

summer afternoon, the neighbor's house exploded. I stood
for a long time holding
my mother's hand at the kitchen window

where I still stand.
Back here, we live on nitrogen. It's dead
quiet except for now and then
the sound of a clumsy girl
playing a violin.

Twilight, mostly, in the winter.
Morning mostly spring.
A pick-up skids into the roses, *flowers and hormones, cradles*
     and narrow graves.

The past is an orgy
in a military state.
We're running through the radiation, playing
Crazy Eights, swimming
naked in the Lake

of No More Surprises, starry-

eyed and bored
out of our fucking minds,
standing stupidly beside
the sneezing man on the subway, the one

with the virus that will take our lives, or

eating stale cake and taking
vows we never break. And all

through the dreaming and accounting,
the commerce and desire, there is

this one wan fellow wandering with his cocktail across
    the lawn, going

from guest to guest
introducing himself as awe.

IV. X Ray

Through the blue
forest, in the twilight, behind
the white vibration of your bones, a woman
named Marie

carries a glass of water, which glows. She

bears it carefully. She knows

you're broken. The party-
goers are frozen, the music's over. It was

eerie, always, the music, wasn't it? And the flowers
so brief and pale. The beautiful

boys and girls, intangible as song. Who

knew, all along, it could be seen through?
That there were swans
and sails floating
in the lunar dusk inside you?

That the air you breathed
and the water you drank
turned into aria,
and mood?

She knew.

Mr. Mitchell

October 24, 1929: The day was overcast and cool. A light north-west wind
blew down the canyons of Wall Street, and the temperature, in the low
fifties, made bankers and brokers on their way to work

button their topcoats around them.

The day was overcast and cool.
A ship was leaving
or coming in. A woman

was standing on the deck of it, watching
the Statue of Liberty become
clearer, or disappear. A small

boy in a side yard
chased a red ball into the road. A speeding
car stopped
without hitting him, and both

the boy and the driver began to cry. There were

carillon bells on a campus. Books

on a shelf
written in Latin. A girl's
pet rabbit
slept in a cage
made out of chicken wire: It

was having dream as blank as a mirror turned toward the sky.

Steel, Telephone, and Anaconda. The leaves

had begun to turn in the trees—orange and brown and the
    dull red
of that boy's rubber ball. Then

it all began to fall. Two, three, five,

ten points at a time, and a fog
began to rise

slowly around the past, loving
every second of it, but swallowing and gasping, like
a needle passing through its own eye, and Mr. Mitchell ran

frantically out the front door
of the National City Bank,
and into the future, where

I was standing in line
behind the others, trying

to buy something, which

already existed in the place I was standing, the last
woman in a long
line as he ran past, never

noticing me, never even imagining

my longing, and how
all my American life

it would be born twice—

in the wanting, and in the having—

something sweet and cold and obscenely
expensive, a thin straw stuck casually
into the crushed ice.

Credit Card in My Hand

A child cries in a field of grass
between one place and the next.
There is no border
but horizon.
No wind or sky on the map.

A woman lets her hand
skim the surface of the river.
Her boat is going to drift

for years on this calm water
before it reaches the falls.

A thing with credit
and without debt.
Like the effect of autumn air on children
Like vanGogh's *Starry Night.*
Like four dumb onions

in a mesh sack in the cupboard.
Or the corpse
shelved with the others

in the damp catacombs—

this one wearing a wedding gown,
and a veil over
the truth's face.
Or the shepherd

who claimed his sheep
climbed to the top of a hill one day

and never came back down.

Sennacherib of Assyria

The city and its houses, from its foundation to its top, I destroyed, I devas-
tated, I burnt with fire, I dug canals, I flooded with water, and its very
foundations thereof I destroyed . . .

then I got tired,
tired like a child,
put my head on the kitchen table and sighed.

Some mornings, a wild bird flies
blindly around inside my body, bumping
its way naked through the halls, knocking
the small things off:

The snapshots and clocks.
The crucifixes drop
softly onto the wall to wall.

In another room, Godzilla makes
his familiar echoing empty noise, a dry
and throaty cry
that seems to emanate
from somewhere behind and inside

the monster he's become.

Godzilla! a scared man shouts.

Honey, turn that down.

I feel sorry for Godzilla, my son said once. *He wants a friend, but now*
everyone's against him

because he broke their town. Stumbling

into a skyscraper, grabbing
hold of the nuclear reactor, he brings
the whole thing down.

Last May, a teenage girl
jumped off the overpass
onto the interstate . . .

If only she'd waited one day—

The woodcutter shifts
the weight of his ax
from one shoulder
to the other . . .

The playground full of unexploded mines

Resentment, boredom, spite,
or an unfortunate accident like

the woman who saw
miraculous visions
in the water at the bottom of her cup,

but, grown weary of her own thirst,
drank them up.

My Son in the Cereal Aisle

Today I am one of a hundred mothers
who loses her child at the grocery store.
I am pushing a silver cart piled
high with the gold of the poor.

Weighing grapes. Counting ears of corn.
When I turn around I see

that where the child was standing
by the apples
there isn't anyone, just

a smudged red light which
rises from them muttering, *how*

large is fear? where do I feel love?

Once, I saw a housecat
at the zoo, caged
with a wild cat, who

paced at the bars, snarling at the babies, while
the housecat yawned in a bit of shade, her
eye a green slit into her mind,

and I thought I heard it say, *I'm*

company. If you want to, you can look at me. But

I'm not like this other one,
back and forth, back and forth,
chewing matchsticks, making plans.

Go ahead. The door is open. Thief, come in. I promise

I'll draw this feather
across your throat before I draw the knife

I leave my cart behind.
Everything packaged.
Everything priced.
The fauna in families. The flora
according to its kind.

Teeth in the grass.
Roses growing in a mine.

The world has come to an end.
Some mothers rise to heaven.
Some claw at the linoleum tiles.
Great bushels of grapes and grain

are dumped into our arms from the sky.

I turn up the cereal aisle

and there I glimpse our children dancing
in and out of the furnace
uninjured by the fire.

Small Boys Petting Caterpillar

Somewhere, a god
is handling our hearts.
Wonder can kill, accidentally, what it loves.

It's summer. The ditches
are full of fish-scales and glitter. Also
the sepulcher, the tomb, the pit. Someone
has scraped them out of the air

with the dull edge of a knife. Someone

has told them to be gentle, and now
their little hands are light as prayers. If
they breathe, their hands will float away.
The music of dust in water.

One of them is trembling. One

is bouncing with his legs crossed.
Perhaps he needs to pee.

Above us, on the highest limb, a dangerous piece of fruit
     dangles.
A teenage girl is stepping

all over the sunshine in her tennis shoes. Perhaps

that piece of fruit will simply
drift into her hands.
It did, for me. Swiftly,
but with wings.

And the caterpillar

is a word, a soft bit of star. Oblivious, our hearts. Could
that word be *faith*, or *trust*, or is it

some other word which means
to let go in ignorance, or to hold one's breath and hope?
And would that word be *love?*

It doesn't matter because
we're helpless in the hands of what does.

Please

Stay in this world with me.

There go the ships.
The little buses.
The sanctity, the subway.
But let us stay.

Every world has pain.
I knew it when I brought you

to this one. It's true—
the rain is never stopped
by the children's parade. Still

I tell you, it weakens
you after a while into love.

The plastic cow, the plastic barn.
The fat yellow pencil, the smell of paste

Oh, I knew it wasn't perfect
all along.
Its tears and gravities.
Its spaces and caves.
As I know it again today

crossing the street
your hand in mine
heads bowed in a driving rain.

Mud

This is spring's grim silk —

mud, and a love deep enough
to swim or drown or bathe
or be born in. My cat is gone, *my*

tearful sleeve, my lazy one. How long? This

is the exchangeable
merchandise of love —

wild garlic, broken glass, a hubcap in the mud. My

cat, I see, has been here. Her
French mittens in the ditch, but

she's gone on. How far? This

open field between *malignant*
and *benign.* God

is up there watching
someone crucified. Oh,

not His only son. Not mine. Not

my husband, father, me. God

is watching someone
He never noticed before
get nailed to something He'd
mistaken for a telephone pole. Tonight

I'll place a plastic cup of peas, a small
fork, a piece of cheese, and my

whole life like a shield

of fragrant vapor—weightless, shifting—
before the only one in this world

whose loss I couldn't endure.

Once, I drank a spoonful of perfume.

And the cat, the cat's a detail—crooked, impatient, sweet
and also gone

somewhere, I know and loathe it, somewhere
killed or crying, lost
or never noticed
by a very near-sighted God. *I wanted*

to smell like violets deep inside. Once

I wore a short skirt to a dance
and kissed a boy who died
before my life began.

The Juniper
Prize

This volume is the 27th recipient of the
Juniper Prize presented annually by the University
of Massachusetts Press for a volume of original poetry
The prize is named in honor of Robert Francis
(1901–1987), who lived for many years at
Fort Juniper, Amherst, Massachusetts.

Laura Kasischke has published five collections of poetry.
Her third novel, *The Life Before Her Eyes*, was published by
Harcourt in 2002. She lives in Chelsea, Michigan.